Where's That Cat?

by Barbara Brenner and Bernice Chardiet
Illustrated by Carol Schwartz

Cartwheel ·B·O·O·K·S·®

SCHOLASTIC INC.

NEW YORK TORONTO LONDON AUCKLAND SYDNEY

Library of Congress Cataloging-in-Publication Data

Brenner, Barbara.
Where's that cat? / by Barbara Brenner and Bernice Chardiet;
illustrated by Carol Schwartz.
p.   cm—(Hide-and-seek science)
"Cartwheel Books."
ISBN 0-590-45216-9
1. Cats—Miscellanea—Juvenile literature. 2. Felidae—Miscellanea—
Juvenile literature. 3. Picture puzzles—Juvenile literature.
[1. Cats—Miscellanea. 2. Felidae—Miscellanea. 3. Picture puzzles.]
I. Chardiet, Bernice. II. Schwartz, Carol, 1954– ill. III. Title.
IV. Series: Brenner, Barbara. Hide-and-seek science.
SF445.7.B73   1995
636.8—dc20
                                                          93-40722
                                                              CIP
                                                              AC
12 11 10 9 8 7 6 5 4 3 2 1   5 6 7 8 9/9 0/0
Printed in Singapore

First Scholastic printing, April 1995

Introduction

Some have stripes.
Some are white.
Some are spotted
Or black as night.

They all have fur.
They all have claws.
They walk around
On padded paws.

Some are wild.
Some are tame.
Where are those cats?
Come play the game!

Kitten Games

The neighborhood kittens are playing together.
They're all wound up in a game of yarn ball!
It's hard to tell who's who in this pile.
But look hard and you'll see three gray kittens
with black stripes.

It's a Fact:
There are about one hundred different kinds
of house cats.
Gray, striped kittens like these are called *tabbies*.
There are more tabbies in the world than any
other kind of cat.

Cat and Mouse

Twenty cats are looking for mice to play with.
But mice know that cats can play rough!
The mice are hiding in the grass.
How many mice can you find?
How many cats do you see?

It's a Fact:
Some cats hunt mice for food.
Others simply play a cat-and-mouse game.
The way a cat acts with a mouse depends on
what it learns from its mother.
But playing or hunting, a cat's padded paws
help it to stalk and to pounce!

Scaredy-cat

Cats love to prowl at night.
They're not usually afraid of the dark.
But one of these cats *is* scared!
Its ears and whiskers are pointing down.
Its eyes are round.
Its fur is standing up all over!
Can you find the scaredy-cat?
Do you see what it's afraid of?

It's a Fact:
If a cat is happy and relaxed,
its ears stand up, its fur lays down,
and its whiskers point straight out.
A cat's whiskers are amazing.
They can sense the slightest movement.
If a cat is scared, it will behave like the
frightened cat in the picture.

Parade of the Pedigrees

These fancy purebred cats are strutting
their stuff at the cat show for pedigrees.
A Siamese cat has just won the blue ribbon.
Can you find the winner in this group
of *purr-fect* cats?
(*Hint:* Her eyes match the ribbon on her neck.)

Oriental Shorthair

Abyssinian

Tonkinese

Devon Rex

Persian

It's a Fact:
A purebred cat has a pedigree —
a list of all the purebred ancestors
on its cat family tree.
There are many different breeds of cats with pedigrees.
The Siamese is one of the most popular.
All Siamese cats have blue eyes.
They're very smart cats and can be trained to walk
on a leash.

Russian Blue

Siamese

American
Shorthair

Somali

Scottish Fold

The Tail of the Manx

These romping kittens are playing catch-a-tail.
The one whose tail gets caught loses the game.
But two cats in the picture are sure winners!
Look for them and you'll see why!

It's a Fact:
The Manx cat is famous for having a very short tail,
or no tail at all!
A Manx cat with no tail is called a rumpy.
One with a tiny tail is called a stumpy.

Spooky Cats

It must be Halloween!
Here's a crowd of black cats.
They're hard for us to see,
but they can see us!
Look closely.
Can you find two cats with orange eyes?

It's a Fact:
Cats have no trouble seeing in the dark.
A cat's eye has several special devices
for piercing dim light.
One of them is a kind of reflector.
That's what makes cats' eyes glow in
the dark!

Colorful Cat

Bobtail kittens for sale!
Choose the color you like the best.
The one called a mi-ke (*MEE-kay*) will cost the most.
It's orange, black, and white. It's very rare.
Can you find the mi-ke in this picture?

It's a Fact:
Bobtail cats like this one come from Japan.
They all have short or "bobbed" tails and
they all love to eat fish.
The mi-ke cat's fur always has three colors.
Mi-ke means "three furs" in Japanese.

Those Wildcats!

This tabby cat is lost far from home.
It has just seen a family of African wildcats!
These cats look tough, so tabby has decided
to hide.
Let's hope these wildcats don't find this
little house cat! Can you?

It's a Fact:
The tabby cat may not know this,
but it has found its roots!
African wildcats have been
on the earth for thousands of years.
Scientists are quite sure they
are the ancestors of today's house cats.

GGGRRR! Tigers!

There's a mother tiger in this forest.
She has three cubs with her.
Their stripes blend in with the leaves and shadows.
The mother tiger's stripes hide her, too!
Can you find all four tigers?

It's a Fact:
Tigers are the largest cats in the world.
They can weigh 600 pounds — as much as two refrigerators!
All cats are related. So the big tiger and the little house cat are members of the same family.
But unlike most house cats, tigers like to swim.

Lion Pride

Look at those big cats!
There must be 15 lions in that group!
But there's only one male lion.
Do you see him? He's the one with the
mane — the long hair that frames his face.

It's a Fact:
Male lions are the only wildcats that
have manes.
They are also the only cats that live in
groups, called prides.
One or two males are the leaders
of each pride.
The females do most of the hunting.

Who Bobbed the Bobcat?

Three bobcats are out hunting tonight.
One bobcat is up a tree.
You can see the head of the second bobcat.
Can you see the tail of number three?

It's a Fact:
The bobcat is an American wildcat.
It has pointy tufts of hair on its ears
that collect sounds and help the animal
to hear.
You hardly ever see a bobcat.
But during their breeding season,
bobcats can sometimes be heard
screaming in the woods at night.

Dots and Spots

Oops! Things are topsy-turvy in this zoo!
The jaguar kittens and leopard kittens look so
much alike, they got mixed up.
The zookeeper had better check out their spots.
Can you help?
(*Hint:* The jaguar's spots have a dot in the center.)

It's a Fact:
The jaguar and the leopard are both wild members
of the cat family.
The jaguar grows to be a little bigger than the
leopard.
But the main difference between them is their spots.

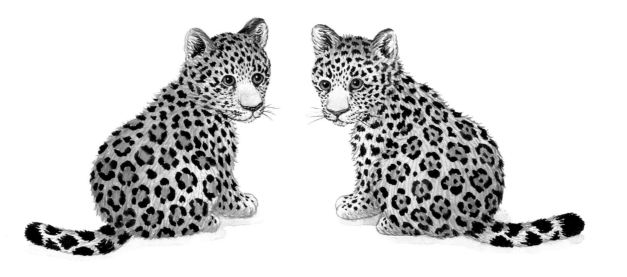

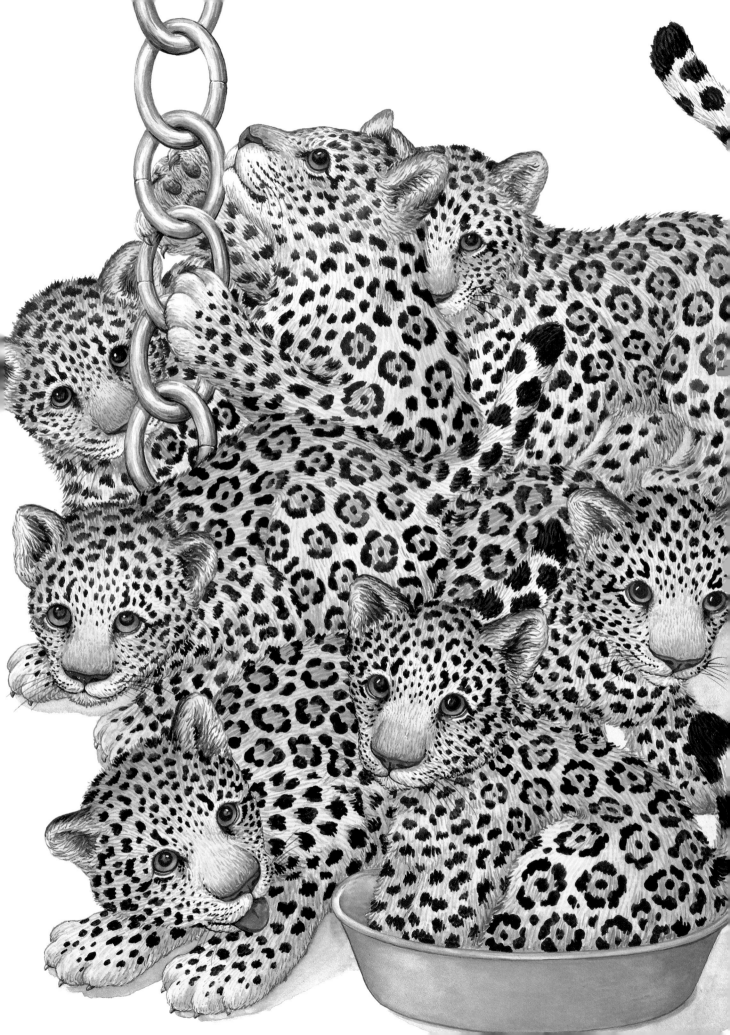

Cougar Cave

A mother cougar and her cubs
are hiding in this cave.
They're the same color as the rocks.
Can you find all three cubs?
(*Hint:* The cubs have spotted fur
and ringed tails.)

It's a Fact:
Cougar cubs, like most cats, are born blind.
They stay with their mother for two years
and learn how to hunt and hide.
After awhile they lose their spots and
ringed tails and look like grown-up cougars.
Some other names for the cougar are —
puma, panther, painter, catamount,
and mountain lion.

Cat Symphony

Some of the cats of the world have gotten together.
Let's see who we know!
There are six tabbies.
There's the Siamese, still wearing its blue ribbon.
Two black cats are all black, but one is not.
Which two cats have the shortest tails?
Which cat is the furriest?

On the wild side, there's an African wildcat!
The male and female lion are sitting together.
The tiger is the biggest cat at the party!
Those two cougar babies are up very late!
The bobcat is making the most noise!
The leopard is looking down on the party.
You can see the jaguar's spots!

(All these measurements are head and body; tail is additional.)

Tiger (*Panthera tigris*)
6′ to 9′; tail 3′

Leopard (*Panthera pardus*)
4½′ to 5′; tail 4′

Jaguar (*Felis onca*)
5′ to 6′; tail 3′

Lion (*Panthera leo*)
6′ to 7′; tail 3′

Bobcat (*Lynx rufus*)
2′ to 2½′; tail 6″

Cougar (*Felis concolor*)
3½′ to 6½′; tail 22″ to 34″

African wildcat (*Felis lybica*)
1½′ to 3′; tail 1′

House cat (*Felis catus*)
up to 21″; tail up to 10″